REQUIEM

A TALE OF EXILE & RETURN

Erel Shalit

il piccolo editions
by

fisher king press

il piccolo editions by Fisher King Press
www.fisherkingpress.com
info@fisherkingpress.com
+1-831-238-7799

REQUIEM: A TALE OF EXILE & RETURN

ISBN 978-1-926715-03-2
First Edition

Published simultaneously in Canada, the United Kingdom, and the United States of America. For information on obtaining permission for use of material from this work, please submit a written request to:

permissions@fisherkingpress.com

Manima, the cover image, is a sculpture by Sonia Shalit. (Dorothy and George Braun Collection, Gothenburg, Sweden.)

Aquarius, the image used throughout this publication, is from a mahzor (prayer book) for the three festivals, printed book, wood engravings, Vilna, 1844 (© Gross Family Collection, Tel Aviv).

This account is entirely fictitious. However, in spite of its fictitious nature, the identities of the characters in this story are real. Professor Eli Shimeoni has agreed to have his story told, on the condition that his real name be disclosed.

Galuth, by Samuel Hirszenberg, 1904.

If anyone would have been present in that clean and tiny room in the small hostel in the heart of New York the day Professor Shimeoni arrived, watching him as he sat almost catatonically on the bed, his legs barely touching the floor, his cap awkwardly sitting on his head as if put there by a caring nurse on a schoolboy rather than a man in his mid-fifties, his small unopened suitcase next to him as if he needed to protect it with strengths he no longer possessed, or as if the suitcase somehow squeezed itself quietly to his side so that it could protect him – if anyone had seen Professor Shimeoni sitting on the simple bed in the warm but alien room, they would have seen a picture of resigned defeat.

But no one was present. Nobody was there to observe that bitter smile that held back his emotions, when he thought, "how ironic, this bed is hardly better than those furnished by the Jewish Agency once upon a time to immigrant hostels that had been scattered around the country." "Once upon a time," he repeated to himself, not sure if it was a dream or a nightmare, a fantasy or an anxiety attack.

No, there were no witnesses. The defeat remained the private failure of Eli Shimeoni.

Incidentally, Eli was short for Eliezer. However, since he had never managed to figure out if the meaning of the letters that made up this given name of his was that God would be helpful to him, or if he was to be God's servant in a scheme of contradictions that his philosophical mind could not grasp, he had formally shortened it to Eli.

Professor Shimeoni felt lonely and abandoned, like a redundant survivor. At fifty-six, he looked like an old man. Even when he was a child, people had told him he was an old man, but now, not a trace of doubt remained. He profoundly experienced himself as the last survivor. It seemed to him that everybody had already left before him. He came to think of that abandoned town he had once visited, driving down there into the desert, driven primarily by an obsession to see and sense an external manifestation of his own feelings of abandonment, of being left behind. He had always believed that the barren land of the desert was better suited for expelling the scapegoat and abandoning the unfortunate than for the dreamers of divine prophecies and the growth of oases. The fata morganas were, indeed, fairy mirages, inverted illusions, unrelated to desert reality.

The young had left the desert town as soon

as they could, leaving their unemployed and worn-out parents behind. Once the little kiosk at the small piazza at the center of town, with coffee, chairs and a lottery machine, had been like a Persian Palace of Hope, a real kūšk.

But the feathers of hope no longer circled the air, as if impatiently waiting to be followed by the lucky and daring ones, departing for the dream of a new life, a better future. No, the feathers had all fallen to the ground, the shaft had lost its barbs. Even the feathers had lost their hope. No longer projected into the future, hope had merely become a relic of Professor Shimeoni's favorite tense, which he cynically ascribed the negligible value of a threepenny, the PPP, past perfect progressive – "they had had hope – had they not had?"

No one in town could any longer define that thing called hope. Unemployment pay had run out with the rusty water in the taps, wasted, dripping into the sand. On the pavement outside the kiosk, the formerly white, now turned gray chairs of aging plastic, had become orphaned. As weeds sprouted up between the cracks, it became clear that the sidewalks were no longer made for walking. Days of decay no longer took turns with nights of despair, because in despair, there is still some voice trying to call out, however futile. No, even despair had now become orphaned, replaced by an empty void of apathy. Among those who managed to escape, the void was often filled to the brink with restless guilt.

Yes, it was sad, he had thought at the time, as he felt the relief of getting out of the godforsaken town, hastily escaping north. Yet, it was part of global depopulation trends. But now, his sense that everybody had left was different. It felt total, and like desertification, it had crawled in from the periphery to consume the very center of life, people like him, the pillars of society, the salt of the land – those that may not be immune to tragedy, but who conquer the desert rather than surrender to nature.

True, not everyone had left. There were those who remained behind – he thought of the many poor who had no means to get away, and *the baalei teshuvah*, those Masters of Repentance who had returned to the fold of the orthodox fathers. It seemed to Eli Shimeoni that their return to the straight path of God had given them the freedom not to ask any questions. They always knew the answer so well, claiming that "in the War of the End of Days, the War of Gog and Magog, total defeat would precede the ultimate victory over evil," as they knew to repeat by heart.

He had been fascinated by the fanatic obsession with the graves of holy men, whether those scattered over the country, prominently Shimon Bar Yochai at Meron, or those orgiastic journeys by the Bratslav Hassidim to visit the grave of Rabbi Nahman in Uman, or Uriah the Hittite in Iraq – what a thrill! Coming himself from a somewhat religious background, he often wondered about the fundamentalist need of doomsday fantasies, their need to split the world in good and evil, a "pure" world in which the "impurity" of the "evil other" will be persecuted and exterminated, without the simple realization that this means that if I succeed in my crusade, I will remain trapped as the evil exterminator. On the other hand, he found it almost as difficult to accept the post-modern credo of "everything goes," as if everything is of equal value and there is no Truth – except, that is, beyond the absolute truth that there is absolutely no truth above other truths. In fact, there must be no other truths besides the one truth of many truths.

His head turned, as it often did when he tried to understand matters that probably were much more complicated than he thought.

First his children had left, gone abroad to study. One had taken up a prominent position at the University of Stamville, while the other was doing gender research at the Institute of Harback. Then his wife had followed, accusing him of being a fanatic and an archaic idealist, or derogatively calling him silly and stubborn, an obsolete Zionist. Friends and colleagues had discreetly taken farewell. Initially they would apologetically say, "if things ever change, you can be sure I will be the first one to return home. After all, there is nothing like Israel, and you can not really extract Israel from an Israeli." But then, people became increasingly forceful and determined as they said goodbye. The cultured ones would say with bleeding hearts, "this is not the country we prayed for," and the self-proclaimed prophets would plainly tell him, "everything is collapsing, there is no future here." Some would reinforce their doomsday prediction, relying on historical evidence that an independent Jewish nation could not survive more than a hundred years.

But what struck him the most was, that everything was so everyday-like. Nothing special, nothing particular to notice. So similar to Elie

Wiesel's pastoral description, "I left my native town in the spring of 1944. It was a beautiful day. The surrounding mountains, in their verdure, seemed taller than usual. Our neighbors were out strolling in their shirt-sleeves. Some turned their heads away, others sneered."

That's all. Nothing unusual. Only the mountains were taller than usual. And yet, when as a young man Eli had read those few lines, which he had memorized ever since, the impact on him had been shocking. In lieu of immanent mass murder, there was an uncanny sense of the ordinary, sensed by the mountains that were moved more than people were. As man became smaller, the mountains became taller. The uninvolved, the willing or unwilling bystander, may, or may not, have struggled to avert the conflict that the disruption of the ordinary entailed. The victim, on the other hand, would already have been transported away from the reality of a beautiful day in spring, however, not yet fully trampled down by the boots of the octopus.

Friends and colleagues had ever so often told him that his attitude reminded them of the Jews in Germany in the 1930s, who were blind to the writing on the wall, refusing to believe that the most cultured of enlightened nations would turn into history's worst beast. Those

Jews of enlightened blindness were convinced the storm-wind would subside, the storm-troops would slow their pace, the God in whom they no longer believed would soon Pass-over. Unable to realize that their spiritual presence in Germany had come to an end, they could not imagine that their physical existence, as well, was over. How had they not been lured into the shadowy abyss of destruction! By exaggerated trust in culture and authority, so called 'prominent' German Jews were all too easily persuaded to take the train to 'Theresienbad,' without realizing that their choice of "Wunschen Sie Bitte – please, would you like" a room at the lake or by the city square, was simply part of the Theresienstadt make-believe.

But there were those who saw through the game of deceit. The poet Leo Strauss wrote, in Theresienstadt, what in its subtle simplicity is a spectacular poem, Als-Ob, *As-If*. Eli S. tried to recall his own translation of the poem, which went something like:

> I know a little tiny town
> a city just so neat
> I call it not by name
> but call the town As-if

Not everyone may enter
into this special place
you have to be selected
from among the As-if race

And there they live their life
as-if a life to live
enjoying every rumour
As-if the truth it were

You lie down on the floor
as-if it was a bed
and think about your loved one
as if she weren't yet dead

One bears the heavy fate
as-if without a sorrow
and talks about the future
as if there was – tomorrow

Those days, in that clean and tidy, tiny little room at the hostel in the heart of New York, Professor Shimeoni certainly seemed to be a refugee.

He recalled how members of his family had crossed Europe by train merely a decade-and-a-half or so before he was born. His grandmother, who at the time was fifty-six, just like he was now, had gone from Vienna to Theresienstadt, and was then transported onward to the last station, her final destination.

Some of his family had arrived in time to the Land of Israel, before the Germans opened wide the gates of "work and freedom," and the British white-papered the certificates, preventing entrance to the mandate they supposedly had.

There were those, like him right now, who had made it to the America of Golden Safety, "De Goldene Safve," as one of his uncles used to say in an English as broken with Yiddish as his own with Hebrew.

His associations, however, went further back into the more distant past, to the Jews who had left those same shores at the eastern edge of the Mediterranean for exile and Diaspora.

He imagined the men and the women, the elderly and the infants, crowding the sandy shores, boarding the ships that set sail across the sea. That very moment he understood why the passionate longing for home had anchored in the Jewish soul, and why the sense of the soul's exile wandered like a shadow behind every Jew. Those shores he knew so well were no longer full of playing children or of smiling lads and teasing maidens and suntanned tourists. In his mind he saw, rather, the pushing and the screaming, the anxiety and the desperate clinging together for comfort, as the fate of dispersal lie in wait for the Jews of the Destroyed Temple, soon to board the ships of salvage for a future of pogroms and persecution.

Now, just like then, many had stayed behind, perhaps mostly those that had had no choice, scattered in little towns and villages around the country, under foreign rule. He imagined the day of upheaval, when Rabbi Yochanan ben Zakai, youngest pupil of Hillel (who is known for the ethic of reciprocity, "That which is hateful to you, do not do to your fellow. That is the whole Torah, the rest is the explanation"), was smuggled out of Jerusalem in flames in a coffin during the Great Siege. Yochanan understood that as Jerusalem was on fire and the Temple destroyed, an historical era had come to its end.

He established the Council of Yavneh. While he himself still resided in the Land of the Fathers, this would be the beginning of Rabbinical Judaism, and millennia of Jewish Diaspora. For Eli S. this was *the* picture of a fugitive, of a refugee in the making. Exile and return had been wavering back and forth for centuries, even before the destruction of the Second Temple. But the year seventy of our common era was a moment close enough in time so that he could touch it, or that was recent enough to touch him. He could almost stretch his hand out across the short distance in history, and grab the side of the coffin, as if he himself carried Rabbi Yochanan ben Zakai out of the burning Jerusalem, across the hills and the fields down to the coastal plain, for future wanderings to leave their trails on the maps of world history.

Sometimes there had only been a few who remained, while at other times they returned to gather into quite remarkable communities, perhaps more of the mind than the flesh, in a barren country, reborn centuries later during the era of Zionist renewal and prosperity.

His tranquil ruminations about exile and return, rebirth and destruction, were suddenly interrupted when Professor Shimeoni felt his entire body flush, feeling as if he had been stripped of his clothes, to bare nudity. He recalled the words of the Norwegian philosopher Jostein Gaarder, of "Sophie's World" fame, who in 2006 wrote, "We do no longer recognize the State of Israel. … We laugh at this people's – the Jews – fancies and weep over its misdeeds." Then, foreseeing the fulfillment of his wet dream he excels in triumphant compassion, exclaiming "Peace and free passage for the evacuating civilian population no longer protected by a state. Fire not at the fugitives! Take not aim at them! They are vulnerable now like snails without shells… Give the Israeli refugees shelter, give them milk and honey!" Not a far cry from Hamas leader Dr. Mahmoud Zahar, whose diagnosis says, "Israel has no historical, religious, or cultural justification, and we will never establish relations with this cancer."

Quickly, quickly, help get rid off the cancer! I accuse, I accuse you, Jostein Gaarder, and with you I accuse those European intellectuals, with whom I have always felt affinity, who collaborate with the grand deception, 21st Century Faux, in which the boundaries have been blurred between empathy of the heart and apocalyptic hell, between depth of mind and simplicity of thought, Shimeoni exclaimed to the absent audience. This is when you can conclude, with the ease with which you brush crumbs off the map, that "Israel simply has no right to exist," a fact which the author of an opinion piece in the *Guardian* always has "considered central to any genuine peace formula."

So simple, so subtle, he thought, not really knowing if he had calmed down; peace will prevail when Israel is destroyed, tranquility will prevail in the Holy Land when the Jews have left, as the claim goes. The evil hiding behind the deceptive logic of preconditioning "genuine peace" with denial of the right to exist nearly escapes perception. And if Jostein Gaarder believes it is a result of Israel's bad behavior, as he claims, he is wrong, Professor Shimeoni insisted. It is the other way around; the reluctance to accept Israel among its neighbors and among the nations, lies bare beneath the surface. "We have left the Middle Ages behind," says Gaarder the philosopher, and goes on to "laugh uneasily" at the Jews with their "funny stone tablets, burning bushes, and license to kill." "The license to kill does not belong, nay, it does not pertain to

the Jews, no, they have no such license!" Shimeoni cried out agitatedly. Not only in the history
of the past, nations have killed Jews and other
people, still others keep killing, and some nations threaten to kill, with particular fervor the
Jews, without losing their license to exist.

How easy is it not to believe what you want
to believe, to believe the subtleties of your own
projection, he thought. How easy it was to accuse the brutal Israelis for the Jenin massacre,
which never took place. He recalled how at the
time, a journalist from Neue Zuricher Zeitung,
who had been there, plainly told Shimeoni, "Everybody knows there was no massacre, but you
can't write that."

Honestly, and perhaps naively, Eli Shimeoni
had asked, "why can't you?"

Then, coming to his senses but still embarrass-
ingly naked, Professor Shimeoni thought quietly
to himself with a bitter sense of irony, "besides
the fact that I neither want Gaarder's milk nor
his honey, and anyway prefer beer to milk and
herring to honey, it's not only the paranoid Jewish mind that is obsessed with the scenarios of
our end, but obviously the minds of the most
enlightened philosophers' as well."

He recalled the words of Chaim Potok, who so
poignantly gave voice to that collective concern,

"To be a Jew in this century is to understand fully the possibility of the end of mankind, while at the same time believing with certain faith that we will survive." Living in Israel was certainly living at life's edge, at the edge of survival.

Bitter irony turned into sour cynicism, as Professor Shimeoni reflected on the word "certain." He was convinced that an eloquent writer such as Potok had purposefully used the ambiguous word *certain*. "Is there a word more *un*certain than certain?" he asked himself rhetorically. "Did Potok mean that we could be sure, could be *certain* in our faith that we will survive, or did he mean that we may have some, a bit, perhaps a certain bit of faith that we will survive?"

Eliezer Shimeoni did indeed have a certain, a very certain faith that the Jews would survive.

His belief was that the Jews thrived at the edge of pathology – their individual pathology, but also their collective pathology as a people. But, as accounted for so well in the annals of history, they primarily thrived as the target of other peoples' pathological projections. Looking into the mirror of history, looking back all these decades, at all those ordinary Germans, Jews and Europeans, Eli wondered, how come they did not see?

For far too many years after the Shoah, many Jews and especially Israelis, arrogantly looked down at their brethren who had, so it seemed, submissively been led "like sheep to the slaughterhouse," victims not only to ineffable brutality and demonizing projection, but also to systematic deceit – and then, after the catastrophe, to the silence of suppression and denial, and the words and the voices of depreciation.

Had not the ordinary German, covering the gamut from willing collaborator to frightened compliant, been infected by years of indoctrination and selective information? "When I myself look into the mirror," he said to himself, "it is somewhat embarrassing to admit that, perhaps, I may have wished Chamberlain success in his mission of appeasement. I have always had a soft spot for Neville Chamberlain. He pronounced himself to be 'a man of peace to the depths of my soul,' and I believed him, and I like to see myself as a man of peace to the depth of my soul."

With the Nazis five years into power, and aware of the danger that Hitler would drag all of Europe into a terrible war, Chamberlain's policy of appeasement seemed so sensible for a cultured nation. I can truly understand him, Shimeoni said to himself, when he rhetorically asked why the British should be "trying on gas-masks because of a quarrel in a far away country, Czechoslovakia, between people of whom we know nothing."

"It sounds at least as civilized as that recent question," Eli thought, posed not so long ago by French ambassador Bernard, who asked why the world should be in danger of a third World War because of, as he said, "that shitty little country?"

You may not need to be reminded, but September 1938 he signed the pact with Hitler. To bolster the conviction that Europe would be saved by the appeasement agreement, French

PM Daladier hailed Goering as "a man one can do politics with." Why not a nice dinner, as well, and perhaps un cigar, monsieur? October 1, 1938, *The Times* praised the "Declaration of Peace in Munich," concluding that the Munich conference "has not only banished the danger of war over the future of Czechoslovakia," but it "has speeded up a new and a better era in European relationships." Thank God for The Grace of Times! Upon his return, proud and popular Chamberlain waved the paper he signed with Hitler and declared he had brought "peace with honour. I believe it is peace for our time."

And Professor Shimeoni, for one, would have made his way to Heston Airport and applauded him upon his return, because he is a man of hope and peace.

Thus, he told himself, "I cannot blame the passively collaborating German, and can only admire and feel a deep love for those who dared to see and those that dared to act." Particularly he thought of Wickard von Bredow, as the example of exceptional heroism: As County Officer (Landrat), he received the order, November 9, 1938, to burn down the synagogue in the East Prussian town of Shirwindt, just like all the synagogues in Germany that were to be destroyed during the next few hours. Von Bredow put on his German Army uniform, said goodbye to his wife, and, as Martin Gilbert reports, declared: "I am going to the synagogue to prevent one of the greatest crimes in my district." He knew he risked his life and that he could be sent to a concentration camp, but added, "I have to do this."

When the SA, SS and Party members arrived to set the synagogue on fire, he stood in front of the synagogue, loaded his revolver in front of the group, showing them that they could only get into the building over the dead body of the Landrat. The synagogue in Shirwindt was the only one in the district not destroyed.

Eli Shimeoni wondered, "Would I have dared to trespass the prohibitions, would I have dared to buy from a Jewish store? I hope so, but the honesty that fears evoke, makes me wonder. If I would have been a 1938 German, may I not have looked the other way, avoiding the shame and the guilt gazing back at me in the store owner's eyes of shattered glass."

And he knew very well that pathology is always stronger and more powerful than sanity, just like hatred settles into scorched ground, while love forever remains aloft, like letters written in the clouds. Does not Father Death eventually swallow every one of Life's Children?

Did not Papa Sigmund prove psychoanalytically that death in fact becomes the very goal of life? And yet, however harsh and firm the ground, "is not nearly everything a question of mind," he thought? "Is it merely a geographical issue if Israel is a Mediterranean country or a nation in the Middle East – which anyway is a relatively recent term? What is it anyhow, the Middle East or the Near East, or are they the same? Or is it a question of where we place it in our mind and consciousness?" What is the location of Israel? Shimeoni considered Israel as anchored in the Mediterranean basin, rather than as a country in the Middle East, which principally was a designation for the lands surrounding the Persian Gulf. He saw Israel as an integral part of the rich and colorful flora and fauna, of the species that made up the Mediterranean cultures, at the junction between East and West.

Those very days in that tidy little room with the little desk where he could sit down and write after he had summoned some of his strengths and managed to rise from the bed and exorcise the apathy of resignation, he did what he always did, and started to scribble down his account of events. He looked back in bewilderment how quickly it all had unfolded. Perhaps it started a year and a half ago, on March 30, when the Arabs in Israel commemorated "Land Day."

"Well," he thought, "of course it started long before." Perhaps it started around the talks in Annapolis – the impressive peace production with its open-ended declaration, followed by a year of "vigorous, ongoing and continuous negotiations," that were ultimately no more than fruitless attempts at reconciliation. President Peres had said at the time that the alternative to Annapolis is catastrophe. Only later would it become evident how right he was, or, rather, how Annapolis and its aftermath could not prevent the inevitable catastrophe. And did not the Prime Minister at the time say, when he went *off* stage yet *on* record, that "the state of Israel is finished" if a separate Palestinian state is not created. The end was certainly on his mind, just like on everybody else's.

Professor Shimeoni tried to organize the order of events, and he jotted down:

For a long time the Palestinian President had threatened to resign, but yielded to American pressure to remain in office. His continuously weakened position, however, was exposed by the humiliating coup carried out by a coalition of Islamic Jihad, Hamas and groups from within his own Fatah movement. Without any resistance, they entered his Muqata compound in Ramallah, pointed their guns and threatened to execute him. After merely an hour or so, a document was signed, and the President was allowed to leave the headquarters of the Palestinian National Authority (PNA) and the West Bank of Jordan for a safer haven. He appeared to be quite relieved from a burden far heavier than what a decent man's shoulders can bear.

Just like their take-over a few years earlier in Gaza, the Hamas, now as head of "The United Arab Coalition of Islamic Forces in Palestine," had swiftly taken control of the previously Israel-occupied part of the West Bank, which had been handed over to the PNA. A day after expelling the President, all Government Ministries and most military bases were in the hands of the Hamas. The little resistance that arose had easily been crushed, as many of the president's loyal forces left with him for Jordan. Having gained experience in Gaza, the Hamas enforced a strong military rule, harsh censorship, and the anti-Israeli messages in mosques and media intensified. During the years of Arafat's and Abbas's leadership, Israel's destruction had been called for on a daily basis in the media and even in the schools. But now the threatening tongues sharpened into swords of heinous hatred; the oft-repeated verses about "the Jews as the scum of evil, the descendents of the apes and the pigs," were broadcast several times a day, as were the calls for volunteers. Hundreds, if not thousands, signed up for suicide martyr missions and for training camps in Iran. Israeli roadblocks on the West Bank, which according to the Israelis had for such a long time been instrumental in curbing terrorist attacks, while they bore the insignia of humiliation and oppression for the Palestinians, were stormed by tens of thousands of civilians. While some carried weapons, there was no need to fire a single shot. The soldiers were just trampled down, and in most instances the blockades were removed within minutes.

Israel responded by sending troops into the Palestinian territories adjacent to Ben-Gurion International Airport, fearing it would come under missile attack. The European Union sent a message to Israel that its response was "out of proportion." The French Foreign Minister condemned Israel of committing "a disproportional act of war with negative consequences."

In Israel, the population had become increasingly concerned. Crisis had of course always been an everyday commodity in that complex country. Yet, surveys now showed that most of the adult population no longer believed that Israel would still exist as an independent Jewish state a decade from now. There were so many other signs – investments slowed down, social unrest and frequent strikes (which always had played a prominent role in the Israeli drama, but now seemed to have a graver impact than in the past). Even in prosperous Tel Aviv, real estate plummeted. People were tired; it seemed as if they just couldn't bear the burden anymore. The vulnerable social fabric, which had been held together even during the five years of massive terror after the failed Camp David talks in 2000, started to rupture. The deep-rooted, annoyingly confident but meaningless mantra "yehiye beseder," don't worry, everything will be all right, had turned into a resigned, defeatist "lo meshaneh," it doesn't matter. Nothing seemed to matter anymore.

Professor Shimeoni registered everything. He

had always paid attention to social processes, even though it was not really his field of specialization. His intuition did not fail him. He felt the direction the wind was blowing, and the Eastern Pneuma, the harsh desert wind from the east, beat him in the face long before the storm settled into visible facts. Many of the country's great talents, in all fields, stayed away for longer periods of time, and he was well aware that he had as many Israeli colleagues in the United States as at home in Israel. But he had never believed he would join them.

In fact, he would never join them. When away from home, wherever he was, he would always remain in transition, as becomes a refugee. He knew that most of them anyway never really settled down abroad, and like him, remained in transition. The feeling of transition was often only exacerbated when they realized that their *children* neither lived in transition, nor shared their sentiments for the place called Home. How Eli Shimeoni ridiculed those leftist peaceniks who became pathetic patriots, telling him their heroic army stories, well aware that unlike him until quite recently, they never had to do reserve duty in that dusty desert, endangering their lives, or the lives of their children. Yet, in spite of their ludicrous nationalism, somehow they seemed to free themselves more easily from the bond that constituted the psycho-genetic code of almost every Israeli. At least they pretended. In his arrogant way, which verified his Israeli identity in spite of his otherwise rather European manners, he claimed that just like you know at home, in Israel, when tragedy and terror strike by the sentimental, bittersweet patriotic songs played till exhaustion on the ether – you can equally guess what year someone had left Israel by the nostalgic songs pouring out on his tape recorder or CD Player.

Wandering off in reverie, E.S. came to recall some of those great men, such as Heine, who at the end of their days tried to search their way back, to remember where they came from. True, Heine had said that there was no need for him to return to Judaism, "for in fact I have never abandoned it." Shimeoni was not really convinced, yet felt embarrassed to argue with good old Heinrich. His prophecy that where books are burned, they will ultimately burn people, was inscribed at the very centre of his psyche. Just like "God was quite delighted by His composition of the woman's body," as Heine said, Eli could not but be delighted by H.H.'s Song of Songs. And who knew exile better than Heine, "Does not the oak grow higher in one's land? Do not the violets sway more gently in that dream?" And was it not Einstein who had said that we Jews had been "too eager to sacrifice our idiosyncrasies in order to conform?"

His thoughts swayed gently, soothingly, in his field of associations. He wondered what one forgets when straying away too far, and what one remembers when departing on unpaved roads in new lands.

He recalled how he once had asked a rabbi,

whom he had befriended, about the sin of forgetting. The rabbi had told him there is always a way back, and told him a Talmudic story about the rat, the sky and the well, or was it perhaps about the wise woman?

Once upon a time, a girl was going to her father's house when she lost her way and wandered off far from town. She was very thirsty, and so, seeing a well with a rope attached to it, she climbed down it to drink. But she could not get back up. Cry and scream as she might, no one heard her. At last, a man passed by, looked down at her, and asked if she was a human being or the demon in the well.

"I guess that for many a man, even a petite woman may seem to be a big demon," mumbled Shimeoni in an attempt not to interrupt the rabbi.

"I'm a human being," she answered, weeping and begging to be rescued. "If I save you," he asked, "will you lie with me?"

Shimeoni could not restrain himself, and said, "seems there's got to be sex not only in a psychoanalytic story, but in a rabbinical one as well."

"Yes," she answered, giving him her word that she'll have sex with him. So he labored to get her out of the well.

"Ha-ha, see how you get the men going, even in Talmudic times!"

Why are you surprised? Did you not read the Scriptures? Was not our King David an adulterer? Without letting himself be disrupted, the rabbi continued.

Having labored hard to pull the young lady out of the well, the man said, "Now keep your promise," because he wanted to go to bed with her.

She was a clever girl, however, and asked him, "Where are you from?"

He proudly told her where he was from, and that he was from a priestly family. "I too am from such a family," said the girl. "Can it be that someone from a holy family of God's priests could wish to work his will with me like a beast without even a marriage contract? Come with me to my parents' house and I'll marry you honorably and chastely."

The man agreed to this, and they pledged being faithful to each other. "But who," they wondered, "will be witnesses to our oath that we shall marry each other?" And so they decided to have as witnesses the sky, the well – and a rat that happened to pass by.

You see, said the rabbi, the *sitra achra*, the other side, of which we want to know nothing – the sky of the Lord gets dark and cloudy, and in the well we believe is full of wisdom, evil may lie in wait and drown us in our own stupidity – that other side always hangs around us, and follows us like a shadow. What witness is more trustworthy than the sitra achra, which holds so many secrets, even secrets that we have forgotten, and secrets that are hidden from ourselves? What witness may be more suitable than the ugly rat that passes by as if by chance, who tells us not to forget the illnesses it may bring if we forget?

Then the man, and the girl he had just saved and promised to marry, went their separate ways. The girl kept her pledge and turned down every one of her many suitors, who came to town to marry her. Once a young gentleman, wealthy, learned and wise, virtuous and of a distinguished family, arrived from afar. When he saw such a beautiful young lady, and from such a good family, he sent the matchmakers, as customs obliged, to her father to ask for her hand.

The father was delighted to hear who the young man was and said, "Let me ask my daughter ("for those times, quite a liberal father," thought Shimeoni), and I will give you an answer."

"Daughter," he said to her harshly, (hmm, not so liberal, after all) "until now I have respected your will and not insisted that you marry any of the young men who have courted you. But your latest suitor is handsome, wise, wealthy and virtuous, and I want you to listen to me and agree to be his wife, because we will never find a better match for you. Such good fortune is too precious to let slip through our hands. I insist that you marry him whether you want to or not."

Those were her father's words, and the girl's mother followed suit, and also begged her to be reasonable. And so when she saw that neither parent would relent, she pretended she had gone mad, and tore her clothes and those of anyone who came near, so that they would leave her alone.

"Sometimes madness is the way out when there is no way out," Shimeoni muttered to himself.

She even took to walking the streets barefoot, tearing her clothes there too, and throwing stones at whomever she saw. Then no one in the whole town asked for her hand anymore, because everyone thought she was crazy.

"You see," said the rabbi, "it is not that people who go mad necessarily walk around nude in the streets, but madness is sometimes the nakedness, the naked truth behind our clothes, behind our external garb."

Meanwhile, the man to whom she had promised her loyalty – well, he forgot all about his oath, married another woman, and had a son by her.

How easy men forget! Ahh, now he comes to the issue of forgetting! Had not the sin of forgetting been the issue that triggered the rabbi's story?

The boy was a fine lad who was his parents' pride and joy. One day, however, while he was playing in the yard, a rat –

"Oops, here comes the sitra achra, the 'dirty' side again! You forget, you repress, and then it jumps up in front of you – or worse: what the parents have forgotten, will often turn up in the lives of their children"

– a rat came and bit the fine lad to death. His mother mourned his strange death greatly, but after a while she conceived again and bore another son. Yet, the fate of this boy too was fatal; he fell into a well and was killed. Then the woman was stricken with great grief and wept bitterly, refusing all comfort. "God is just," she thought to herself in her sorrow. "There must be a reason for what He has done," she said to herself.

"Well, I would need to interrupt you," said the professor to the rabbi. "Perhaps I should not enter into a theological and existential argument with you at this moment, but I am not sure I agree with this seemingly very wise woman; I am not sure that God is always just, but who am I to know who or what God is?" Was it not Elie Wiesel who said that God's presence, or his absence in Treblinka remains a forever insoluble problem? Did he not add his sharp observation that one day an explanation will be found, on the level of man, how Auschwitz was possible, but on the level of God, it will remain an eternal mystery?

The rabbi continued without being interrupted, And so she called her husband to her room and said to him, "My dearest, perish the thought that God should do anything unjust. If the Holy One, blessed be He, has punished us twice with the death of our little sons, we are guilty of some sin."

Again, sorry to interfere with the story, but I am not so sure it works that way: sin, guilt and punishment; but since I am neither theologian nor philosopher, and I am certainly not a great moralist, said Shimeoni, so I shall let this wise woman speak for herself.

"We must think of what it may be," said the wife, "and since I have thought and thought and found nothing, I want you to think too.

Please tell me, my dearest, if you have any old misdeeds to account for, so that we may correct our ways."

"I haven't made up my mind yet whether I admire her conviction of being guiltless, or if I think she is a bit pretentious, but I admire her sincere way, and how she insists her husband should also do the job of self-scrutiny," commented Shimeoni.

The man's sorrow was such at hearing his wife's words that, making a great effort to recall all his deeds, he suddenly remembered the oath he had taken to marry no one but the girl he had labored so altruistically to save from drowning in the well. After all, he was an honest man, so he told his wife about it. Justifying God's ways she said to him, "My dearest, let us divorce each other lovingly and peacefully. Go to that girl whom God set aside for you and keep your pledge to her so that innocent souls need perish no longer and the Cup of Bitterness need not be drunk again."

All right, I do in fact agree, and believe that unawareness and avoiding reflection – of which we all may be guilty – have a tendency to cause harm in others.

And so the two of them went to the rabbi and were divorced, and the woman went her way, no one knows where.

The man then set out for the girl's town. When he arrived and asked about her, he was told that she was mad. "Nonetheless," he said, "please tell me where her father lives." And going to the man, he said, "I understand, sir, that you have an unmarried daughter. Would you agree to let her be my wife?"

"How painful your words are to me!" said her father. "It is true that I once had a precious gem of a daughter, but for quite some time she has not been in her right mind, and she cannot be a wife to any man."

"Still," said the man, "I want to marry her. At least be so good as to take me to her."

"Very well," said the father. And he took the man to his daughter, who behaved like a madwoman.

"My dear, don't you know me?" the man asked, reminding her of what had happened. "Try to remember the day when I found you in a well in a lonely field."

"Tell me about it," she begged, beginning to come to her senses. So he told her the whole story, and when he was done, she was restored to her right mind, and she recognized him and said, "Because of you and of my pledge to you, I have suffered all these years, but you see that I have kept faith."

They then went to her father and mother and told them the story too, and what great joy there was! A wedding was held, and the two of them were married, and they had children and grand-children and lived happily ever after.

That of course is an ending in order to end the story, which after it ends only continues, merely as the beginning of a new story – "but I got your point," Eli told his friend, "about telling our story, and hearing our story, and knowing there is a witness to our story; a witness who does not run away but survives to tell the story, and prevents us from forgetting, from leaving in the belief we can discard what we left behind and what our commitments are."

But I wonder, do we need to tell the story of the sitra achra, the story of the other side, as well? Do we need to tell the safra achra, the other story, the story not told, the story in the negative, the story that hides underneath, the story of loss and despair, of fear and of hatred, do we need to get lost on our way, to fall in the well, in order to find ourselves? Can we become righteous only if we contemplate doing wrong, going wrong? Can the gold only be found in the grey, the splendor of the world only in the sew-age rat?

While he had no reason to be arrogant, Eli Shimeoni did feel sarcastic toward the somewhat sad and futile attempts, such as Derrida's effort late in life to come to terms with his Judaism. Truth was, Shimeoni essentially agreed with Derrida on many points, such as his interpretation of Abraham's covenant with God of circumcision. The Divine Father's archetypal scar inflicted by generations of fathers of the flesh on generations of consent-less Jewish boys seemed to Professor Shimeoni, as indeed to Derrida, to be a repetition-compulsion, rather than the profound internalization of memory. He recalled Yosef Hayim Yerushalmi's epic work *Zakhor*, wondering if the Jews don't merely repeat the trauma when they cross the desert every Passover – outside of the Land of Israel even repeating the hegira a second night, perhaps to ensure that the Jews of the Diaspora do arrive at the Promised Land... "Does not compulsive repetition constitute the dangerous engine of fundamentalism?" he wondered, "in contrast to an enlightened process of internalized memory, in order to liberate the trauma." Is this not the very opposite of that monumental cultural transition when the knife is taken out of Abraham's hand, turning the ac-

tual, concrete sacrifice of Isaac into the accultur-
ated representation by his Binding, the *akedah*?
The knife need not actually cut, in order for man
to humbly bow before the transcendent image
of God. Shimeoni adhered to Einstein's view of
God, as when he says that the religious attitude
is the knowledge and emotion "of a knowledge
of the existence of something we cannot penetrate, of the manifestations of the profoundest
reason and the most radiant beauty," and when
he expresses his belief in the God of Spinoza
"who reveals himself in the orderly harmony of
what exists, not in a God who concerns himself
with the fates and actions of human beings."

The *meaning* of sacrifice, rather than its exe-
cution, is made sacred by proxy and by under-
standing, rather than deed. So why was there
a need, from which, in spite of his doubts, he
could not free himself, to physically cut, in order to preserve the covenant? Eli wondered if
his phobic fear of knives, and his fainting spells
when seeing blood pour out of the body from
even the slightest cut, may have begun on this
fateful eighth day of his covenant with God.
Out of sheer fear, Eli sometimes thought that
in self-castrating circumcision he would have to
cut off the El, the very God in his name, and
remain with a mere "i," sometimes inflated to a
capital I.

Remaining a tiny "i," his mind wandered around the hills of Jerusalem, his thoughts circling down to where the city reclines, attempting to hold the tension between the harsh stones and the reflection of multi-colored light. From its heart, the ancient city pounds and pulsates along the arteries of its narrow lanes and alleyways. If you put your thumb to the chest, he thought, just left of centre, you will feel the exhilaration, turmoil and pain around the Temple Mount. Within the tiniest of physical space, barely covered by the fingerprints of your thumb, within a mere square kilometer, one third of a square mile, you find the sacred basin of the Shekhinah, the Son of Man and the peacock's tail of al-Buraq, The Flying Horse.

Behind the Wall of Tears, the timeline descends from the mosque to the Temple of Jupiter to the pigeon-sellers, to the Temple and yet the one before, right down to the altar of worship and sacrifice. It is here, at the point of the needle, where history and legend merge at the very hub of indistinguishable uncertainty, that the awe-inspiring drama of the sacrifice of Isaac supposedly took place. What terrifying, formidable lesson did God want to teach Abraham, when he told him to go forth to the land of Moriah and offer his son Isaac for a burnt offering?

Abraham does not question his God, with whom he has sealed a covenant. He binds his son Isaac and lays him upon the wood of the altar he has built. The son submits to the father, Isaac to Abraham, and Abraham to God – a weakness of character? Hardly, since Abraham has already proven his capacity to leave his father's house, and no less, when he argues and negotiates with God to spare the sinners with the righteous in Sodom.

Perhaps Abraham did not ask any questions because this was simply his adherence to the ancient practice of surrendering the first-born to the gods? The Scriptures tell us Abraham offered up his "*only son* Isaac." Consequently, some Muslim scholars claim that not the little laughing one was to be sacrificed, but Ishmael the first-born, who was the only one who could be the only one of Abraham's sons. Did not the God of compassion hear the lad who cries of thirst, expelled from his father's house into the desert?

"Is it not a common practice to this day for many a father to sacrifice their sons on the altar of this or that divine expectation, of one or another ideology or firm conviction?" Eli Shimeoni asked rhetorically, when suddenly he started to tremble, as he wondered if this was what he was doing to *his* children. Had he sacrificed them on the altar of his beliefs? Just to keep a mad project going? Just because he thought there was value in keeping an ancient culture alive? Did not our national poet Yehuda Amichai lament the death of Stalin – mourning the leader of a country that recognized the State of Israel, emperor of socialist equality, the victor over Nazism, rather than celebrating the death of the dictator, murderer of millions? How easily do we all fall prey to false beliefs, only in retrospect realizing how mad we were!

He wondered if Abraham argued with Terah when he left his father's house and went forth to the land unto which God would lead him? What doubts pounded in his heart when he put the burnt offering upon his son, for him to carry the wood, some say cross, of his own sacrifice? Was this the wood of the sacred grove that so meticulously had to be cut down, as when Yahweh commands, "build an altar to your God upon the top of this rock, and offer a burnt sacrifice with the wood of the Asherah which you shall cut down?" Without being asked, was little Isaac to carry the Lord of Hosts' mighty struggle against Asherah, the goddess of the grove, on his shoulders? Was he to be sacrificed, bound to the mother of the morning star and the king of the evening, the mother of the twin brothers Shahar and Shalem – yes, Shalem, the Canaanite king-god and mythological founder of Ir-Shalem, Jerusalem?

The Biblical account is the skeleton of a drama, for the reader to flesh out with feelings, and to be dressed in the garb of interpretations. There is not a word of dialogue between father and son as they ascend the mountain of worship – is it the awe of fate, the brevity of speech when walking straight into inescapable tragedy, or is it the focused silence when you walk the line, stretched to its limits across the cosmic abyss? Or maybe it is the chilling coldness of mechanically executing daily movements, when you submit to invincible catastrophe, as when rather than waiting for the five o'clock bus, you are lining up at Umschlagplatz for the next train to Treblinka?

Is this the story of the Jews' submission to the father, in which the instincts of the sons bend to the fathers' discipline, with the rabbis as a Halakhic fortress cementing the power of God, the Father? Or is it the callous need of fathers to castrate their sons, who on the one hand embody their future and bring the prospect to "multiply exceedingly," but who on the other hand, by their very prime and youth, seem to hold the sword that separates the future from the past, determining who by water and who by fire, who will rest and who shall wander, as the poem recounts our disastrous fate on Atonement Day?

In some legends, he recalled, Satan tries to prevent Abraham from carrying out the sacrifice. In his role as adversary, instigating toward consciousness, Satan introduces some healthy doubt into what otherwise seems to be passive submission. But in Biblical reality, it is only when the angel calls upon Abraham not to slay his son, that he lowers his hand, and puts away the knife with which he was ready to sacrifice his beloved son. He has passed God's test of devotion, and the ram is offered in place of Isaac.

But has he passed the *human* test of devotion?

Himself renamed by God, Abraham received the honor of naming the place, and he calls it Adonai-yireh, because the Lord sees and has been seen, in complete (shalem) awe, yireh-shalem. Thus, the awe of the innermost light, which sees, and blinds when seen, radiates from the heart of Jerusalem. Yet, is this perhaps not the foundation of civilization, when the image graven in stone, is projected into the light?

Truly, he repeated to himself, the binding of Isaac signifies this striking cultural transition from literalness to symbolic representation. God

told Abraham there is no need for complete sacrifice, only a sacrifice of the complete (shalem),
in order to be seen (yireh), to be recognized, to
be named, to become completely human. He
will suffice with sacrifice-by-proxy. Rather than
being trapped in the harsh reality of actual deed,
reality can be transformed into images; rather
than slaying the flesh of the son, the soul can
expand by the creation of images that *r*epresent
reality. By substituting the sacrificial animal for
the actual son, the story of the *akedah* represents
the separation of meaning from act, which is es-
sential to culture and civilization.

But war is the destruction of representation
and civilization, said Eli to himself, thereby ar-
guing with Heraclitus that War is the Father of
All. The tragedies on the battlefield are all too
real and irreversible, and the essence of trauma
of battle and war and Holocaust, is the loss of
the representative symbol – all that remains is
the hellish repetition of trauma. Nothing represents the loss of symbolization better than the
survivor from hell who holds on to a dry slice
of bread. In hell, there are no mirrors and no
images, no images in the mirror, only the bare
walls of suffocation. In the cruel reality of war,
the knife is raised and the angels circle above,
repeatedly descending, attempting to divert the
hand that holds the knife from descending upon

the son, until the angels have all gone, and the son is no longer bound but sacrificed, the knife ripping out the soul of life and Isaac laughs no more.

The numinous light of Jerusalem shines too brightly during the day, softened only when gathered by the moon at night. The harsh stones that burst in holy rivalry at daytime turn inwards in pain during the night. And one day one might wonder, where will they all have gone, the sons and the fathers, and the angels that descend from heaven to prevent the knife from descending further, to its conclusion in the terror of the heart, the angels that prevent the binding from becoming the sacrifice of Israel, the sons who struggle with the angels.

"Oy vey, to where did my mind wander away," he called himself to order, the way he often had to do when sinking into reverie. He returned to his argument with Derrida:

But as Derrida *circumfesses*, he would reach the end of his days without even knowing Hebrew, without knowing what he called the unknown grammar of the source, of what he strikingly thought of as Home, the origin from which even Derrida himself emerged. And then, so characteristically, Derrida turns his lack of knowledge into an asset, shredding excessive humbleness, claiming he, no less than God, could have invented the covenant of circumcision, as he did in his *Circumfessions*. "What typical Jewish hubris!" he thought, "even those reluctant Jews find it difficult to forsake that sense of being The Chosen One," and he burst into a liberating laughter, realizing that he had not laughed in a long time.

"It is so easy to throw off the yoke," he thought as he put the pen to his lips as was his habit when he paused for reflection, "so easy, so expected, to repeat that original act of Abram and to get thee out of thy country, and from thy kindred, and from thy father's house, and from thy identity, and from whatever thou may believe in. Nobody, thank God, neither God nor the rabbis, can any longer force you to believe in any God or follow any rabbi. You neither need to believe, nor speak the language, neither remain, nor belong to anything but yourself. Yes, Rilke said it so well, that we need to search for the stranger in order find the way Home. But to search the way back, the long way Home, whether to the Scriptures, to the mysterious Hebrew language, the labyrinth of Jewish culture, to the subtle and always vulnerable Jewish identity (whatever that may be) and to your land, is so much more difficult than to leave it all behind, whether in blessed memory or in blissful oblivion."

Could a language thrive without being rooted in the ground? Did not Hebrew lose its soul and mystery when confined to be the language of prayers? As his father used to tell him in his limited Hebrew, he knew quite well how to speak with God, but not to order coffee and cake in Hebrew. But what about Yiddish? Was that not the language of the dispersed Jews, or at least many of them? And Ladino? Well, he thought, Ladino was a refined tongue, suited for romances and cuisine, and Yiddish fit well to overcome the insurmountable obstacles of everyday, to pinch the marrow of life. But the mystery of Hebrew could not be grabbed if purely written on the parchment in the house of worship – it needed unpretentious coffee and sugar in order to tell its hidden stories.

"Well," he said to himself, "the road home, to trace the path back to one's roots, to whence I come, was a much longer and more painful road than the departure and the road away from home." He wondered if, as a collective venture, it now had come to its end. Feeling himself carried away he wrote, "The sense of national undertaking, Israel as a platform and container of collective aspirations, as a vibrant society, as a Hymn of Hope as well as the violin's sorrowful stroke, as a frightening battlefield and as a mad rollercoaster between euphoria and mourning –would that living reality now come to an end, merely to be inscribed in history?" While *the wisdom of writing*, which is the original meaning behind the Hebrew word for prophet, *Navi*, marked the transition from dwelling in, as Chaim Potok had said, "the obscurity of the past" into history as a "living record of the cultures of man," writing now may come to mean a transition from living reality to the obscurity of historical records.

"Israel," he wrote in his notebook on the desk in that little room in the hostel at the heart of New York City, not certain yet whether it was a prison or a shelter, a refuge or a mortuary, "Israel was a fantasy." It was the collective effort, a great venture that would give material shape to a dream, the dream of return, of returning home—the very opposite of the virtual reality of post-modernity. The dream had kindled the fire in the soul of some of the Jews on the brink of farewell – farewell to the ways of the Father and the traditional customs of the Jews, moving on to the illumination of enlightenment and the radiant sun of socialism, stepping out of the bonds of the past to live the freedom of choosing one's own individual quest and to fly on the wings of new visions, arising from the horizon of a new day. The idea to turn away from Father Sky and redeem Mother Earth had taken shape in the minds and the hearts of some, who thus set out to rejuvenate and re-touch their Jewish heritage – to break away from its garb, yet remain in its fold, rediscovering its ancient soul.

Eli Shimeoni hardly managed to finish the sentence, as his mind wandered off in reverie, and his ruminations brought him, seemingly, to take off in a completely different direction. Only afterwards did he realize the possible reason – his sense of affinity with Kafka's shy personality, and his unfulfilled yearning for his Hebrew soul. Without forewarning, S. found himself transposed more than forty years back in time, walking down Tel Aviv's King George Street, sometime late winter or very early spring, if his memory did not fail him. He headed for Pollack's antiquarian bookstore, which even as a young teenager he frequented as often as he could. For him, the thick and heavy air of old books was rich and wise, a comfort and a relief, a refuge from breathing the thick and heavy air of home, which he needed to escape. Those days, after the war of the days of creation, arrogance was in the air. Everyone seemed to fill their lungs with victory and invincibility. But young Eli kept breathing the air of threat and fear, doubt and concern, the compressed air that lay squeezed like the dust in the corners of his room and under his parents' sofa bed.

The old bookshop granted an escape into a world of history books and timeworn atlases in which he could sail across the sea of time and continents, where fear and excitement and heroism were free and asked no price. It was a world of books that he could browse but never buy, an odyssey that could only be traveled, but never owned.

Sometimes his mind would play out heroic fantasies. However, unlike his schoolmates, he was neither the warrior who saves his country, nor the soccer player who leads his team into the world cup final, triumphantly circling the field wrapped in the national flag while an ecstatic crowd sings the anthem. No, his libido was lit by a raging fire, threatening the shop and its treasures from Heine to Freud as if this was Bebelplatz, Berlin, May 1933. In sharp contrast to his usually slow, pale and shy ways, he would courageously run into the fire and save the most valuable of all the books and atlases and manuscripts.

But that grayish winter day, as he stood outside the window to see if everything was in place, his eyes caught sight of a letter, which must have been put there only days ago. He could not make out the German writing, only that it was addressed to Dr. Brod. His mouth got dry, searching for saliva, his heart pounded and his legs trembled as he entered the store to inquire with the old salesman who might have been much younger than he seemed to be behind those round glasses that always slipped down his nose, who told him that Brod had passed away only a few weeks earlier. Those were years that young Eli would swallow every scrap of paper or piece of knowledge or story by Brod or Kafka. He had even read Brod's novel *Tycho Brahe's Path to God*; though he had found the language difficult, or perhaps simply was too young to grasp, he had been intrigued by the conflict between the old and the new, past thoughts and new ideas. But he felt particularly grateful to old man Brod for being wise enough not to follow Kafka's stupid request to burn his books – how could he want his books to be burned!!! Of course he could not know that books would be burned less than a decade later, but for sure he knew about Hananiah ben Teradion, the second century religious teacher, who broke the Roman law against teaching the Scriptures. When burned alive with his beloved, the forbidden Torah Scroll, he said to his pupils, "I see the scroll burning, but the letters of the Torah soar upward."

Young Eli admired the courage of Dr. Brod, but could not really forgive Kafka for wanting to burn his books – only, perhaps, that he had asked in such a way that Brod would understand he did not really mean it. Eli had even seen old uncle Brod once or twice in the street, and tried to follow him without giving himself away, but was too scared that Brod would notice him and scold him and embarrass him and bring him shamefully home to his parents, so he had always made a detour, avoiding Brod's house on Hayarden Street, on the corner of Idelson.

He often wondered about the friendship between Franz and Max, and so much wished that Franz would not have starved to death at such a young age – just imagine if he would have lived with Dora across the street from Uncle Max! Write one more book, please, just one!

Ever since, E.S. had been so involved, that forty years later, only a few years ago, he would search his way to the Tel Aviv District Court (which so typically was not located in Tel Aviv). Behind closed doors, Judge K. presided over the Brod-Hoppe-Kafka trial. Quite simply and very briefly, Brod's secretary, some say mistress, had taken hold of his personal library and all the treasures – "aah! that's how that letter in Pollack's window got there, straight out of Brod's treasure chest!" Paranoically, Mrs. Hoppe seemed to fulfill K's will rather than Brod's. True, she did not burn the library, she kept most of the treasures away from the public's eye, in contrast to Brod, who had saved them for the world of literature and culture. She managed, as well, to capitalize on some of the manuscripts, shipping them abroad, earning a comfortable sum in exchange for the trials of Josef K. After her death, her already elderly daughters kept pythonian guard of the shrine, only letting the cats roam freely. Hardly anyone would know what remained hidden behind the castle gates, except for an expert from foreign lands, whom Max Brod had given brief and conditional permission to bring his looking glass into the judge's private chamber. He may remain the only living person, who has read at least part of Kafka's unpublished works. According to leaks, likely by this foreign expert, one story is about a rat, one among many rats in Prague's sewage system. But this rat had a complex, golden mechanical device, a precise micro-cosmos built into its mind. When Eli Shimeoni tried to imagine it, he came to think of the exquisite Marie-Antoinette watch. It had taken the supreme watchmaker Abraham Louis Breguet forty-four years to complete this masterpiece of all times. The Queen did not live to see this timeless tabernacle of time, ready to be presented to the world only in 1827, even after Breguet himself had ascended from this world. As Sir David Lionel Salomons, the last owner of the watch had claimed, to carry a Breguet watch is to have the brains of a genius in your pocket.

More than a hundred and fifty years later, the Queen of Clocks disappeared from the Museum of Islamic Art in Jerusalem, where the founder, the daughter of Sir David, had opened her father's collection to the public. Marie Antoinette would reappear twenty-five years later, as mysteriously as she disappeared, having been watched and compulsively cared for by the master thief, until his death.

During a quarter of a century, the glass showcase stood orphaned in the cellar of the museum. Shimeoni often wondered what happened to time in its absence. Was this only a simulacrum of time and temperature, a 823 piece replica in gold and crystal of the sun and the moon and a perpetual calendar – or was it a manifestation of Chronos, whereby Time itself moved the hands of every second? Would time continue only as long as it could manifest itself in this world? Would Time end if its worldly manifestations would disappear? Following Baudrillard, Shimeoni, as well, thought the post-modern image had become its own simulacrum, a representation of itself, no longer in need of something "real" that it would represent. According to the same logic, the tangible had become the creator of its own reality, so that a watch did not only represent time, but created time. That would not be much more crazy than Einstein's claim that the separation between past, present and future really is an illusion, or that matter and energy are the same. Or the idea put forth by prominent physicists Holger Bech Nielsen and Masao Ninomiya, that the crazy collider, which thousands of scientists are working on in the Swiss underground, is sabotaged by the future, – which hits back to prevent the collider and all those scientists from disrupting Time – otherwise, why should the future bother to turn up in the present and interfere with scientific progress?

The wealth of images in the post-modern world are detached from reality, but the human mind is somewhat slow in grasping this. Thus, for instance, distorted images and faked news are believed to reflect real events. We have not come to terms yet with the post-modern fact, that the computer-produced images of this era merely represent themselves. There is very little left of what used to be called reality. Similarly, the tangible, for instance a watch, is instrumental in creating time, to the extent that if the clock would stop, so would time, in the sense we know it.

During those twenty-five years, when the whereabouts of Breguet's Queen were not known, Shimeoni had reconciled with the fact that it was enough to *imagine* its existence for time to continue. But did that mean that if *all* objects would disappear, let's say all clocks and watches and pendulums and sundials and hourglasses that measured, reflected and gave tangible manifestation to Time, time would come to a standstill?

No doubt, the clock-like device in the rat was far more advanced even than the horological magic of Breguet. It did not merely reflect time, but was a kind of world replica, somewhat like the Tabernacle built by Bezalel, who knew the letters and their combinations with which He had created heaven and earth. It was not merely a copy of the entire world, but of whatever took place in the world, not only tracing what was taking place in the universe, but itself an instrument through which the world was created, every moment anew. Even though it sometimes seemed as if Shimeoni's mind did some twisting and turning, he was basically a simple and uncomplicated man, always trying to understand by simple examples. He relied on his rather down-to-earth imagination to fill in the gaps. He thought of the compulsive Jewish religious services. He had always felt ambivalent about the clockwork regularity and the command to recite the same prayers (never mind if nineteen prayers were called eighteen prayers, those small anachronisms of make believe as if there was a free will to cheat a little bit by adding something extra), or the weekly reading of the Torah. The same story every day, the Scriptures divided into fifty-four weekly portions, corresponding to the Hebrew calendar. The exact words repeated at fixed intervals, until the end of time. Everything exactly according to the scheme, repeated, read and re-read in accordance with predetermined cycles.

But it is not only the prayers and the Torah readings that are repeated with such regularity. Even those small gestures, which one may mistakenly believe are characteristic of this or that person, have been repeated and will continue to be repeated, and in every synagogue you will find the one who loves to pray and sway to ensure that his requests and his gratitude and his fears and his apologies will penetrate God, for sure. And you will find the one whose nose always itches, and the one with the nervous smile – nothing truly personal, all and everyone replaceable actors in a drama they did not write themselves.

The play is repeated, staged according to laws

and commands. The Talmud says, "Everything is foreseen, and everything is laid bare, yet everything is in accordance with the will of man." Yet, is not the will of man foreseen and laid bare? The actors change, but the roles of the play remain the same. Did not Freud outline the universal patterns of childhood? Does a child that does not crawl cause us concern? Is not free will merely a deviant delusion? Once the producer, the scriptwriter and the director have set the play in motion, there is no longer any truly free, individual will; we are drawn into one out of a fixed number of roles, without much of a choice, Shimeoni believed, even though he wasn't completely sure, particularly since he did not know if this was his own, individual thought. "Wasn't man's thoughts," he reasoned, "in accordance with the grand watchmaker's will?" Just like the orbit of the planets in universe reiterate and expand the cycles of the rotating wheels of the Grand Golden Clock, somewhat like the infinite replications of Mandelbrot sets, the rat itself was doomed to the life of a rat. In contrast to man, however, the rat refrained from asking any unnecessary questions, demanded no sense of individual freedom, and bowed to its fate of being merely a dirty rat in the sewage system of Prague.

Did man really believe that just because he

could stand upright, he was truly different from the movement of the planets, the regularity of the fractals, or the minuteness of the rat? He, and only He – that is, Man – had a will of his own and could depart from the map of the Great Seafarer? Did not research show how heavily man relies on genes and constitution, how his moods and behavior increasingly depended on the Lord's emissaries in today's world, the pharmaceutical industry? Was it man's task to deviate from the "most sublime harmony," as Wolfgang Pauli, the Nobel Prize winning descendent of Wolf Pascheles, the story teller from Prague, sensed from his world clock vision with its vertical and horizontal circles and pulses – or was it man's task to manifest the workings of the Golden Clock in the most sublime and harmonious of ways?

Eli Shimeoni woke up in a sudden spasm of anxiety. He had fallen asleep, as his ruminations had drifted further away, until he felt they turned against him, attacking his sense of being a free individual, master of his own destiny. It was as if *he* was under interrogation, as Tel Aviv District Family Court Judge K. turned into the head of a giant rat with a transparent torso with a myriad of rotating golden circles and colored spheres. He was struck by awe, mesmerized by the sight, lost all strength in his limbs, unable to move. Was he now caught in a nightmare not his own? A mere actor in the play? What he believed to be his own, free and individual will, his personal determination, his choice and his decisions, his own peculiar thoughts, were they nothing but the manifestation of his allocated role, the text he had been given, none of his own creation?

May it paradoxically be that the fear and disgust evoked by the rat, frees the individual from being trapped in the awe and dependent harmony of the Golden Clock?

Were the efforts at gathering his own thoughts an attempt at escaping the anxiety that otherwise would bind him to the rhythm of the inevitable? Could it be that the fate of Israel was sealed by the grand game of chess, or by the cynical randomness of the dice?

Israel was indeed a dream of great ideas and hopes that materialized by the sacrifice of a few. Always a few, in face of the harsh reality of a land that does not let souls blossom easily, as the Declaration of Independence pronounces. Yes yes, he told himself, many of you know that the pioneers came to make deserts bloom, as the English translation reads, but take another look at the original Hebrew of the proclamation: it says the pioneers made souls blossom.

True, he thought, it certainly was a desert land that was brought to bloom. It was a dream that easily broke down into nightmares, a numen too splendid to grow in the barren desert, a fantasy of freedom and independence and survival and mutual caring that hardened in the face of internal strife and conflict; too many wars, all too pyrrhic victories and all too painful losses. But what about the soul, he thought?

Without soul, there is no water and no liquid, no stream, no steam, and perhaps also no dream, he told himself, almost speaking out loudly. Soul does not have material substance. Shimeoni was reminded of the film *Smoke*, based on a script by Paul Auster. The protagonist, the author's alter-ego, rushes into the Brooklyn neighborhood tobacco shop and asks his fellow customers, "How do you weigh smoke?" They don't manage to resolve the riddle. The story tells us that neither did Queen Elizabeth know how to solve it, when 16th Century poet and explorer Sir Walter Raleigh, who introduced tobacco to England, asked her, "how do you weigh smoke?" Clever as she was, she supposedly answered him, "How can you weigh smoke? It's like weighing air or someone's soul."

Is she not right, Her Majesty, Shimeoni told his absent audience, that we cannot weigh the soul? How can we give the soul material expression? Is the soul not as elusive as the wind? As fragile as a soap-bubble? As transparent as glass? Yet, when present, is the soul not as full of wonder as Iris the rainbow, daughter of Thaumas the Wondrous; do we not hear the Voice of the soul on top of every mountain, and its echo deep in every valley? It is the soul that gives character to the wrinkles of old age; when the spirit is lost, the ageing wrinkles turn into parched furrows.

Sir Raleigh's answer to the question how you weigh smoke, was to weigh the cigarette, smoke it, weigh the ash, then subtract the weight of the ash from that of the cigarette, and there you have the weight of smoke.

When we detract the weight of the remaining

ashes from the weight of the unsmoked cigarette, we realize that *soul* and *spirit* weigh heavier than *matter*, but also that they need the matter of the cigarette paper as a container – otherwise they simply disperse into thin abstractions. And if the soul expresses itself by our individual images, is it then, perhaps, our imagination that liberates us from the prison of predetermined fate? However, if our associations become too free, do we not risk displacing them? Like Freud's friend Fliess who thought he would cure poor Emma from her nasal reflex neurosis by removing the genital spot in her nose – surely, psychoanalysis was the science of imagination, and of imaginary illnesses, and the illness of imagination, Prof. Shimeoni concluded his critique.

On the other hand, a person with a lifeless soul is dead, throws no shadow, as legend says, no dirt and no disgust, no faults and no shortcomings, no perversion and no madness. A person without a soul is like a person without a story, and a country without a story takes itself too seriously. Such a nation has no shortcomings. It is perfect and needs no others. Arrogantly, it can remain neutral even in times of crisis. As Dante has told us, neutrality in times that require moral decisions, is a sin that condemns us to the hottest place in hell.

The realization of "the project," as Professor Shimeoni liked to call the Zionist endeavor and the establishment of the Jewish State, was far from perfect. In spite of the more attractive Sabra-ideal, it had always relied on the pathetic schlemiel, the incompetent and unlucky ones: the dream of return was always accompanied by stories of doubt, failure, irony and jokes, for instance that a Zionist is someone who collects money from someone else in order to send some unfortunate schlemiel to Eretz Yisrael ("jokes? – really, was it really a joke?").

Rather than groups of pioneers raising their heads in visionary gaze, the land collected hapless losers, miserable outcasts, troubled souls and other homeless misfits who had wandered astray. "Where lies the truth," he wondered, "with the handsome pioneer on the poster, or with the contemptible schnorrer, the despicable beggar?" "But isn't that the living part of our people? Is it perhaps those who eternally bemoan the misery and the hardships, for whom it truly is 'schwer zu sein a Yid, hard to be a Jew,' that make our people a living reality," he reflected, "rather than those who sit in their sheltered ivory towers merely reflecting about our existence, those who rhetorically ask, 'do we exist at all?', then claiming their academic convictions, 'Aren't the Palestinians in fact the Jews, while the Jews are

Berbers, Barbarians or Khazars, or whatever'?"

And he was reminded of the tale that a young man had told Zev Vilnay in the early 1920s, that when King Solomon called the people to build the Temple, the lot fell on the princes and the rulers to build the cupolas of the pillars and the stairs, the priests were to build the ark and weave its curtain, the wealthy merchants were to build the eastern side, and the poor and the needy would build the Western Wall of the Temple.

So the princes and the rich men took the golden earrings and the jewels from their wives and daughters, they bought cedar wood for the walls and cypress wood for the doors and olive wood for the lintels and they hired foreign workers to do the job and they had them work really hard so the work was finished quickly. The priests found splendid ways, as well, to have the job done efficiently.

Only the work of the poor took a very long time, for they had no fine things to bring from afar, and the men and the women and the children hewed stone, and with the toil of their hands they eventually completed the work.

When the building of the Temple was completed, and the Divine Presence descended and the Shekhinah decided on its dwelling place, God choose the Western Wall, because "the toil of the poor is precious in My eyes." So when the Temple was destroyed, the angels spread their wings over the Western Wall, and an echo went forth and proclaimed, "Never shall the Western Wall be destroyed."

Israel certainly was a miracle, he concluded his meditation. Even during the second a'liyah, the celebrated wave of immigration at the beginning of the twentieth century, which brought Ben Gurion and the founding fathers and the brave mothers to the land, there was massive remigration and numerous suicides. He knew those stories of the early communes so well; the groups of young people revolting against the Way of the Fathers – an intellectual and a revolutionary, the naive dreamer who inevitably became disillusioned, a psychotic who sometimes seemed to be the only sane one around, and the one who always asked questions, as if there was someone around who knew the answer. They were bound together by a spiritual yearning that sometimes was powerful enough to overcome the harshness of the earth – though more often their spiritual hunger and their passionate desire crashed, smashed into particles of pain and despair on the unconquerable rocks.

The country had always been too hard for almost everyone. And the price of keeping it alive was perhaps too high, not only in the past, but in the future as well. For the last several years he had made it a habit, as the sirens rang out on Remembrance Day for the dead, to recall not only the fallen and the killed, friends and relatives, but to think of those whose time is yet to come. The words of the poet Yehuda Amichai were always on his mind, "The bereaved father has grown very thin; he has lost the weight of his son."

"*Land Day* a year and a half ago had been the turning point," he wrote. It had been commemorated by Arabs in Israel every year since 1976, when demonstrations against land confiscation had been violently crushed by the army and the police, leaving six demonstrators killed. But last year it was different from previous years. Until then, instability in the country had been felt like the subtle trembling of the earth. Now, undercurrents streamed into rivers. The Islamic movement called upon all adult Arab men to join the big march to Jerusalem and gather on the Temple Mount, at the compound in front of the Al Aqsa Mosque. The call spread across the country. Young and old, from the Galilee in the north, the Negev in the south, and from the Triangle of Arab towns in the center of the country, turned up in unprecedented numbers. The call spread across the West Bank as well, and people just started marching.

The security services had presented the Ministries of Defense and of Interior Security with reports, in anticipation of unrest on Land Day and the following weeks. The government was not taken by surprise, but seemed paralyzed. The police hastily set up roadblocks across the country, which the masses just broke through. The border police had been instructed that under no circumstance may live ammunition be used. The memory of the killed demonstrators in October 2000, at the beginning of the second Intifada, was on everybody's mind, and no one wanted events to be repeated. In quite a few places the marching crowds managed to take policemen, mostly policewomen, hostages. Most were released the following day in exchange for demonstrators that had been arrested, except for two hostages. A policeman and a young woman from a human rights group, who, by her presence at a roadblock wanted to ensure that the police refrain from violence against the marchers, had been brought to the Temple Mount area. There they were cruelly flung down to the plaza in front of the Western Wall, together with a rain of stones. Praying Jews, mostly French tourists, were quickly evacuated, and except for these, people suffered only minor injuries.

Palestinians from the West Bank managed to break through the security fence. Widespread laughter swept across the long chain of people holding arms as they, within a matter of minutes, tore down "the wall," the security fence, making mockery of our typical Israeli patchwork, professor Shimeoni recalled in anger and self-ridicule.

Sheikh Ra'ad Salah, Head of the Northern Islamic Movement, had been banned by the Israeli Authorities from entering the Temple Mount area, but protected from the police by the huge crowd that surrounded him, he arrived there safely. In front of the Al-Aqsa Mosque he declared, "This is the beginning of our liberation from the infidels. With pride we take back our holy land, which by historical and religious right belongs to us. The 'Zionist empire' (as he said 'empire,' the crowd burst into mocking laughter) shall soon fall, be a feeble ruin, an unfortunate – but fortunately brief – parenthesis in the annals of history, obliterated by Islam," and he continued to quote from the Hamas charter. "Furthermore," he pronounced, encouraged by the huge crowd, "this will be the gateway to victory in Muslim Europe," and with his voice now shouting, somewhat unpleasantly, Shimeoni thought, to those with sensitive ears, he went on to quote Ayman al-Zawahiri, "Oh Muslim nation in the Maghreb, deploy for battle and jihad! The return of Andalus to Muslim hands is a duty for the Islamic nation! Cleanse the Islamic Maghreb of the French and the Spanish!" And, the sheikh added, "first purify Palestine of the Jews and the Zionists, and tranquility and prosperity will prevail!" Surprisingly, he had quoted from the covenant of the rival Palestinian Liber-

ation Organization. The excited crowd responded by the chants echoing from the past, "Idbah
al-Yehud, Slaughter the Jews." In a two-hour
speech he went on and on. "What Holocaust?"
he asked rhetorically, "There was no Auschwitz!
The holocaust is against our people... we are the
victims. From birth, the Jewish child is nursed
by hatred against the peoples of the world... and
the biggest lie in history, by those liars, is their
claim that their Temple is located under the Al-
Aqsa Mosque... Shame on their false claim that
the Al-Buraq Wall, what the Jews shamefully
call the Wailing Wall, is part of their so-called
Temple..." And the crowd responded, "Let them
wail, let them cry!" While arrested later in the
day, he was released that night, having ensured
the release of all demonstrators in exchange for
the hostages.

That was the day Eliezer Shimeoni started to
panic.

Not that he wasn't fascinated by the beauty
and the wonder of Muhammad's night journey
on his flying horse *al-Buraq*, which had the face
of a woman, the body of a horse and the tail of a
peacock, from the Holy Mosque in Mecca to "the
farthest mosque, al-masjid al-Aqsa," as the 17th
Sura of the Quran says. According to legend, he
tied the horse to the Western Wall of the Temple

Mount – hence the Al-Buraq Wall, from where he ascended to the seventh heaven, where he met all the prophets who accompanied him on his way to Allah.

But somewhat compulsively, or, because he had lost both virginity and naiveté at a too early age, he continued to read the lines that followed, warning the Children of Israel they would be punished, their faces disfigured, visited with destruction, and finally be imprisoned in Hell. While attracted to religious and mythological imagination, whether monotheistic or pantheonic, he became superstitiously scared when the gods turned into graven images.

The opposition was united in condemning the government's failure to handle the situation, claiming it reflected the helplessness of a country without leadership. The parties on the right warned against "this threat to the very existence of the Jewish state," while the left accused the government of rigidity and incompetence in dealing with a dangerous and highly volatile situation. The major threat, they claimed, was not at all from the Arabs, but the disintegration of society, corruption and inequality, and especially the humiliating attitude towards the Arab minority. Arab Members of Parliament accused the government of being "an obsolete remnant of an outdated racist regime." Stormy Knesset debates were repeatedly suspended, as physical violence threatened the House of Representatives.

Compulsively, Professor Shimeoni wrote down all those clichés coming from the right, the left and the centre those days. He seemed to be in the power of his resentment, driven by fear and dismay.

During the week that followed Land Day (or, as the Arab leadership now called it, "Liberation of the Land Day"), calm seemed to be restored. The government had recovered from its paralysis, and initiated talks with different segments of the population. The papers were full of rumors and speculations. The ministers were openly suspicious of each other, leaking accusations and, particularly, various embarrassing details about each other. People were unusually thirsty for juicy gossip, which perhaps had a soothing effect, slightly calming the epidemic anxiety.

The mood among the ministers reminded people of Moshe Dayan, once the ultimate image of the Sabra, who at the beginning of the Yom Kippur War in 1973 felt we were on the verge of the "Destruction of the Third Temple."

The editorials were written from different angles and perspectives, but were all united in expressing grave concern about the situation. It was obvious to all that the calm, which had been restored rather quickly, would not last long. Rumors spread that the army would call up reserves in large numbers over the coming year. Many people were deeply shaken, increasingly concerned about the country's future and its very existence. Petitions from all political orientations were distributed, competing for signatures and space in the newspapers.

Without trust in the country's leadership, people increasingly searched for personal solutions. For years, whoever had been able to obtain a foreign passport had discreetly tried to do so, but now the lines in front of Western embassies became longer by the day. When people planned for vacation, they tried to find cheap accommodation for a possibly longer stay. One prominent left-wing Member of the Knesset announced his resignation and intention to leave the country together with his family. He said his love and loyalty to his country remained firm, he saw himself as a patriotic Israeli, did not fail to mention his military record, but he was obliged to ensure his children's future. This caused a public outcry, leading him to retract his decision, but it soon became known that he had already sent his children abroad. On the other end of the political map, there were groups that declared this was the time to strengthen the settlements in the territories, with or without the government's consent, and if need be, they would declare the independent *State of Yehuda*.

"Another stage in the decline," he thought, and continued to register the events.

Then, two weeks later, it began all over. This time it no longer seemed so spontaneous. It was as if there had only been a tense anticipation of the signal or the event that would trigger the unrest. This happened one night when a previously unknown group, "The Warriors of Judith," put up posters in practically every Arab village in the Galilee, with the threatening message "Save Yehuda - Revenge on Holofernes." The Arab leadership called this a provocation with clear intentions; "We are not going to be beheaded like Holofernes, the government is out of control, Israel can no longer be a racist Jewish state, the state is corrupt." They again called for a march to Jerusalem. This time it was very well-organized. Approaching the centre of the country, tens of thousands of demonstrators, arriving in rented buses, turned west towards Tel Aviv, while others continued to Jerusalem. At ten a clock, before they reached their destinations, Hezbollah fired a long-range missile that hit the abandoned Pi-Glilot oil depot, just a few hundred meters north of Tel Aviv's northernmost quarters. The depot had been evacuated following a nearly-successful bomb attack already in 2002, which had failed only because of great – some say divine – luck. It was estimated at the time that if the attack would have "succeeded," thousands of people would have been killed, in fact, three or four times as many as on 9/11. The neighbourhoods of northern Tel Aviv and sensitive security facilities in the area would have been wiped out.

That afternoon, Eli recalled, Nasrallah gave a speech, in which he told Israelis to leave the country, "because your end is near. Palestine will soon be liberated, peace and tranquility will prevail, but you must not pollute its soil with your presence. The sanctity of Al-Quds and the prosperity of the country require there remain not a single Jew on a single grain of the sand of Palestine. We have a great many surprises ready for you. You have no warriors, you have no strength, your struggle is lost. Go home! This is not your home! I tell you, go away! Go away and stay away! If not, your end will be bitter."

Several moderate Arab leaders raised their voice in concern, "See what is happening in Gaza among our own brethren! Civil War and a ruthless regime!" referring to the oppressive regime that enforced its rule and Shariah law by brutal force and indiscriminate violence against civilian Palestinians, and the take-over of the West Bank, as well, by Hamas. However, they were quickly silenced, and in one case, the mayor of one of the Arab towns was stoned, after calling for cooperation with the Jews.

Meanwhile, tens of thousands of demonstrators arrived in Jerusalem and Tel Aviv. It turned out that many policemen had simply remained at home, exhausted from the events of the last few weeks. Tel Aviv's central Rabin Square and the surrounding streets filled up with demonstrators and banners, "Palestine for the Palestinians," "One Palestine," "Free Palestine." Young boys climbed every pole and every pillar, raising the Palestinian flag. Soon the crowd started chanting "Tel Aviv, Tel Arab, Tel Aviv, Hill of Falastin."

"That day everything changed," Eli Shimeoni wrote in his notebook, as if everything did not change every day. Many Israelis increasingly felt like strangers in their own land, as if the ink of the Balfour declaration faded by the day.

From that day onwards, Ahmadinejad made it his habit to repeat three statements with only slight alterations, "We are a peaceful nation," he said, adding, "We have nuclear capacity and missiles that can reach any target," and "Israel is a pariah state; if Europe made the Jews suffer, the Jews should be given land by the Europeans; the Palestinians and the Muslims should not suffer just because Europe doesn't want the Jews." He would then conclude with an emotional call, "Bismillah, in the name of Allah, Bismillah Muhammad, as the aura of green light surrounds me, in accordance with my contract with God, my mission is to pave the path for the glorious return of the Imam Mahdi, may Allah hasten his reappearance, and in the battle between good and evil, the Promised One will fill this world with justice and peace."

Aahh... Ahmadinejad! Was he not Jewish, or at least of Jewish descent? Those Jews, ha, they turn up everywhere, willing to sell their soul as court Jews. Or as converts, they deny their own people to prove their new loyalties. Ahmadinejad, what a glorious name, the virtuous race! Certainly more aristocratic than Sabourjian, the cloth painter or the carpet weaver. Guided by divine prophecy, his parents obviously could foresee his splendid mission! In a few simple, formal steps, the weaver becomes virtuous, unaware that the virtue is in the weaving, that the thread of life is spun on Clotho's spindle. Wagner the anti-Semite and musical genius from Leipzig, whose music still is rarely played in Israel, was afraid he was Jewish, and we "understand," don't we, Hitler's aversion to the Jews, when we "know" that his mother was a Jewish whore. Perhaps we merely need to look deep into the crystal ball of psychologizing, and everything becomes transparent. With only a hint of empathy, we understand how the evil projection and the need to persecute the Jews originate in the need to split off from the detested roots, to ensure the cleansing of the soul from the infectious, cancerous poison.

There may well be truth to the psychological explanation, thought Shimeoni, just like the
logics of paranoia. And perhaps the grammar of
paranoia validates the psychological explanation, thought the philosopher. There is no need
at all for factual basis as regards their Jewish descent; Wagner believed his stepfather Geyer was
his biological father, and suspected, mistakenly,
that he was Jewish (oh, horrendous fate!). Fear
molds truth into falsehood, fear creates the facts
of threat. The fear of infection, a repressed inner
sense of impurity, a soul plagued and torment-
ed by the possibility of contaminated roots, the
sickening danger of contagious descent, "day-
enu, enough already!" Get the crumbles off the
table!!!

He wondered if perhaps Israel and the Jew,
today serve not as the complete stranger, but
rather as "the similar other," and thus a target of
both classical anti-Semitism as well as its post-
modern kin? For the classical anti-Semite and
for the fundamentalist, the Jew is that *Despised
Other*, who may come too close and thus infect
with his evil, "The Jews of yesterday are the evil
fathers of the Jews of today, who are evil off-
spring ... the scum of the human race 'whom
Allah cursed and turned into apes and pigs...'
These are the Jews, an ongoing continuum of
deceit, obstinacy, licentiousness, evil, and cor-

ruption..."

For the post-modern anti-Semite, however, the Jew and the Israeli may represent the *detested similar*, he thought, who is in conflict with that *truly other*, who warrants respect and whom I desire to reach out to. "I can project what I reject or detest in myself, such as colonialism, racism, militarism onto that 'similar other,' thus relieving myself of the need for self-scrutiny," he thought. This similar other is difficult to deal with psychologically; Freud spoke about the narcissism of minor differences. The need to emphasize the difference requires that the dark, threatening shadow be split off, projected onto the otherwise threateningly similar other.

Since post-modernism emphasizes multiple narratives rather than truth, the result may sometimes be a dangerous mixture of the freedom to lie and the respect of evil, rather than knowing right from wrong and honest compassion with the victim, Professor Shimeoni concluded his meditation on the subject.

It seemed Ahmadinejad was biding his time. Intelligence confirmed that Iran had the bomb, or at least was very close. Having learned from the Israelis, the Iranians enforced a policy of deliberate ambiguity as regards their weapons capacity, maintaining they had already reached nuclear capability for peaceful means. Both Iran and Syria had greatly expanded their stocks of chemical missile warheads. Russia and China warned Israel of severe sanctions if it would attack, and the government had realized that an attack most likely would miss the target(s), and serve as pretext for counter-attacks on all fronts. There was a widespread feeling that the day of the bomb was coming closer.

Tel Aviv, known for its vibrant night-life, now saw hedonistic farewell parties for friends leaving, and parties celebrating "Gog and Magog," "Doomsday," and "Who will turn off the light at the airport?"

Missiles and rockets were fired from Gaza, often from schools and mosques, with the Israeli Air Force trying to target the militants. At one occasion a school was indeed hit, killing six small girls. The case was brought to the United Nations Security Counsel, which, surprisingly to many despairing Israelis, did in fact condemn the killing of civilian Israelis (in the course of time, just like during the events of 2000-2005, Israeli hospitals and schools, places of entertainment and worship, had been hit. Suicide-bombers now seemed to favor kindergartens and old age homes). However, "this could under no circumstances serve as a pretext for unnecessary and indiscriminate violence against the civilian Palestinian population, including children." Libya and Pakistan were to head a special United Nations Human Rights delegation to investigate Israel's frequent breaches of international law. Egypt and Jordan decided to freeze diplomatic relations.

While previously a few rockets and missiles had been the daily barrage from Gaza on Israeli towns and villages nearby, now not only the range and the precision of the missiles had been greatly increased, but at least thirty rockets were fired daily. One hit the oil depot in the Ashdod port's fuel storage facilities, causing severe damage and closure of the port. The town was temporarily evacuated.

In the north, the Hezbollah started to fire missiles on a daily basis. They were careful not to fire from positions south of the Litani river, in spite of having taken over the Lebanese army.

The UNIFIL troops had been evacuated long ago – in fact, at the ceremony handing over the territory to Hezbollah, the UNIFIL commander praised "this important charity organization." However, their missiles were precise, and occasionally they fired chemical warheads, which they had received from Syria. While usually refraining from massive missile attacks, they hit homes and buildings in the northern towns of Nahariah, Ma'alot, Carmiel and Kiriat Shmonah almost daily. The psychological damage, both here and in the southern towns and villages, was severe. Cities nearly emptied out, becoming ghost towns, with only the very poor remaining behind, spending most of the time frightened and despairing in crowded and neglected shelters.

After nearly half a year of continuous bombardment, things changed. Again, "The Warriors of Judith" served as catalyst. They now entered Arab villages, carrying out pogroms, destroying trees and livelihood of the Arab villagers. "You set fire to our forests," they said, "and you shall be punished for your pagan worship," they exclaimed, quoting Judges 6:28: "... behold, the altar of Ba'al was cast down, and the Asherah was cut down that was by it." A young local Arab leadership emerged, calling for people to "Raise your heads, raise your legs, Carmiel and Kiriat

Shmonah are Palestine, Oh Arabs, oh noble sons, your blood is in my blood, Palestine is Arab, it is our history, our identity, our future, and we are the disciples of freedom."

Groups of Arabs then moved in to squat in the many flats left behind by the fleeing Jews. Recently, they had taken over an abandoned kibbutz.

The situation in the country reminded people of the Arab riots of 1929 and the revolt of 1936-1939, only much worse. This was truly a great uprising. It was a continuation of *The Second Intifada Uprising* or *The War of Terror,* during the five first years of this century, and seemed to bring it to its conclusion. The internal unrest, shaking the country at its very foundation, combined with the military attacks across the border from Lebanon and Gaza, with a threat that had as yet to materialize from the increasingly unstable West Bank, and with the daily threats that were voiced from Teheran, made life increasingly unbearable. People were afraid to go out in the streets. Tel Aviv was crowded with refugees from other parts of the country. Roads were occasionally blocked, especially in the north, by Arab demonstrators, who would sometimes check identity papers and force Jewish drivers to abandon their cars, which then were set on fire – as had happened already back in the uprising after Camp David, more than a decade earlier.

The helplessness, the lack of leadership, the sense of dead-end, and living in the shadow of the threat of nuclear destruction; yes, the threat was enough, there was no need for Ahmadinejad to implement catastrophe, "which would have left the land inhabitable for the Palestinians," as Professor Shimeoni reflected. The threat was enough to drive the Jews away; the *threat* of the bomb generated the nuclear *reality* that made the *explosion* superfluous.

Eli Shimeoni raised his head for a moment, not realizing the time that had gone by, sitting at the desk in his tiny, tidy little room, pondering over Herzl's Zionist manifesto. "The Land of Israel of Herzl's fantasy was not the *Alt-Neu Land* he had called it in German, the old-new country, but rather the Hebrew *Al-Tnai* (on condition) Land – not the Motherland's unconditional embrace, but a land full of conditions, *a conditional land*, entirely provisional."

He understood that the very idea he had adhered to, a win-win situation with two peaceful states side by side, Jewish Israel and Arab Palestine, had not materialized, and would not come into being, though he had not let it inhabit his soul, because it meant the final defeat of a humane and peaceful solution. For a humanist like Professor Shimeoni, the thought was unbearable, yet, he concluded, "The triumph of man's spirit, which indeed had made deserts bloom, will have to concede defeat to the cruelty of history."

Eli Shimeoni shook his body, stretched his arms and legs, waking up from his long reverie. As he collected his papers for the evening's lecture, he wrote down a few more thoughts:

This short story of fiction reflects a nightmarish scenario haunting many Israelis, which one way or another could materialize. Israel's existence is endangered by external threats of ethnic cleansing and genocide – terms that we prefer not to apply. But the threat is also posed by moral decline and the neglect of the weak and troubled in society, a society in which the social bond and solidarity are cornerstones. Its existence is also threatened by the sense of division between a rigid orthodoxy, fanatic fundamentalism that sees no other, and denies the existence and the rights of the Palestinians, and those that feel their identification with the nation is lost, spiritually migrating away from the sense of identity with the Jews as a people.

Jews face the question of their physical existence as well as their existence as a nation and a people on a daily basis. This plants fear in the soul of every individual, and sometimes requires the most painful sacrifice.

The Zionist enterprise materialized because of the awareness that crystallized in a small number of people. The very identity of the Palestinians as a people crystallized, as well, by means of a process of consciousness – to a significant degree around a central unifying identity as victims and refugees.

Consciousness defeated the Jewish people during the Shoah – not only the distorted consciousness of the Nazis, but also the denial and demonization that characterized the mindset of many European countries, leading them either to active collaboration or to the silence of the bystander – which, as Elie Wiesel said, hurts the victim more than the cruelty of the aggressor.

Consciousness will determine the future of Israel, and the preservation of Jewish civilization and its cultural heritage. When denial collaborates with demonization in the collective consciousness of the world, catastrophe lies in wait for its victim. However, as Carl Sagan has said, "The benefit of foreseeing catastrophe is the ability to take steps to avoid it."

"We may then ask which steps can be taken to prevent the threat of catastrophe?" was the question Professor Shimeoni intended to ask his audience, since the purpose of his story was to ring the bell of urgency, by presenting a worst-case scenario.

"Is it not paradoxical," he thought, "that the Arabs of the Land are hostages to Ahmadinejad's doomsday calls. As long as they induce hope in him of victory, he need not press the button." He felt this was but one of those enigmatic manifestations of an order he could not really grasp, yet it accentuated his sense of devotion, and his intent to listen to his Inner Voice. He imagined the loneliness of those who once upon a time had really been only a very few, and his heart pounded strongly when he thought of the vibrant industriousness and creativity in Israel, which were so striking in the shadow of genocidal threat.

Suddenly he interrupted his stream of thoughts, and wondered how his words would reverberate in him, were he to listen to his own lecture. Imagining himself in the audience, the remarkable picture of the Sabbath evening service in Bergen Belsen, a few days after liberation, crystallized before his eyes. While the dead and the dying still lie on the ground, the barely living survivors let their voices rise from the ashes into divine Hope, singing Hatikva.

The picture of the survivors from the hell of extinction struck him like lightning and etched itself firmly in his mind. Their voices, singing in unison, streamed through his pulsating veins, his heart beat faster and more strongly. He realized that the course of history changes in a single moment, and with a sense of urgency, he knew he had to raise his voice against denial and demonization, the axis that uncannily linked the One Truth of fundamentalism with the intolerable tolerance of evil. He knew he needed to turn what seemed like predetermined fate into the destiny of vocation. He had to respond to the call of commitment. Consciousness, in contrast to denial, he thought, creates commitment. While the manifestations of consciousness are many, the expression of one's vocation remains individual.

He recalled the words of Ben-Gurion, that in Israel, in order to be a realist, you must believe in miracles. "Was Israel not the miraculous realization and the triumph of the spirit of life, forever hovering over the primordial abyss?" he said in a loud and clear voice, adjusting the microphone. As the lights were turned on, he emerged from the shadow of catatonia, and began his lecture.

Also by Erel Shalit

Enemy, Cripple, Beggar:
Shadows in the Hero's Path
ISBN 978-0977607679

The Complex:
Path of Transformation from Archetype to Ego
ISBN 978-0919123991

The Hero and His Shadow, Revised Edition:
Psychopolitical Aspects of Myth and Reality in
Israel
ISBN 978-0761827245

These and many other fine publications are available for purchase from your local bookstore, a host of online booksellers, and directly from Fisher King Press.

www.fisherkingpress.com

International Orders Welcomed
Credit Cards Accepted
1-800-228-9316 Canada & the US
+1-831-238-7799 International